Barbie™
Big Dreams, Best Friends

Barbie™

Big Dreams, Best Friends

NEW YORK

#2 "Big Dreams, Best Friends"

SARAH KUHN – Writer
YISHAN LI – Artist
ALITHA MARTINEZ – Cover
LAURIE E. SMITH – Colorist
JANICE CHIANG – Letterer

DAWN GUZZO – Production Coordinator
MARIAH MCCOURT – Editor
JEFF WHITMAN – Assistant Managing Editor
JIM SALICRUP
Editor-in-Chief

Special thanks to Bethany Bryan and Beth Scorzato

ISBN: 978-1-62991-616-3 paperback edition
ISBN: 978-1-62991-617-0 hardcover edition

Papercutz books may be purchased for business or promotional use. For information on bulk purchases please contact Macmillan Corporate and Premium Sales Department at (800) 221-7945 x5442.

Printed in China
July 2017

Distributed by Macmillan
First Printing

DOES SHE LIKE IT, WHITNEY?
BARBIE, SHHH...
WHAT IF SHE DOESN'T LIKE IT?
SHE'LL LIKE IT.
HOW DO YOU KNOW?
I JUST DO.
BUT...
I DON'T LIKE IT!

YOU DON'T?
NO...
I LOVE IT!
WHEW!

WHITNEY, YOU'VE DONE AN AMAZING JOB DESIGNING ALL THE OUTFITS FOR MY BIG TOUR!
I LOVE THAT I HAVE A WHOLE LINE OF WHITNEY YANG ORIGINALS TO ROCK OUT IN!
OPENING NIGHT TOMORROW IS GOING TO BE THE ABSOLUTE BEST!
THIS ONE COULD USE SOME EXTRA FLAIR ON THE SKIRT, THOUGH...
EXTRA FLAIR IS BARBIE'S SPECIALTY!
OOOH!
WHAT DO YOU THINK, BARBIE? A BIT OF FRINGE? SOME SPARKLES?
UM... UH...
OR MAYBE YOU COULD DO YOUR SIGNATURE FABRIC PAINTING?
WELL, I...ER...

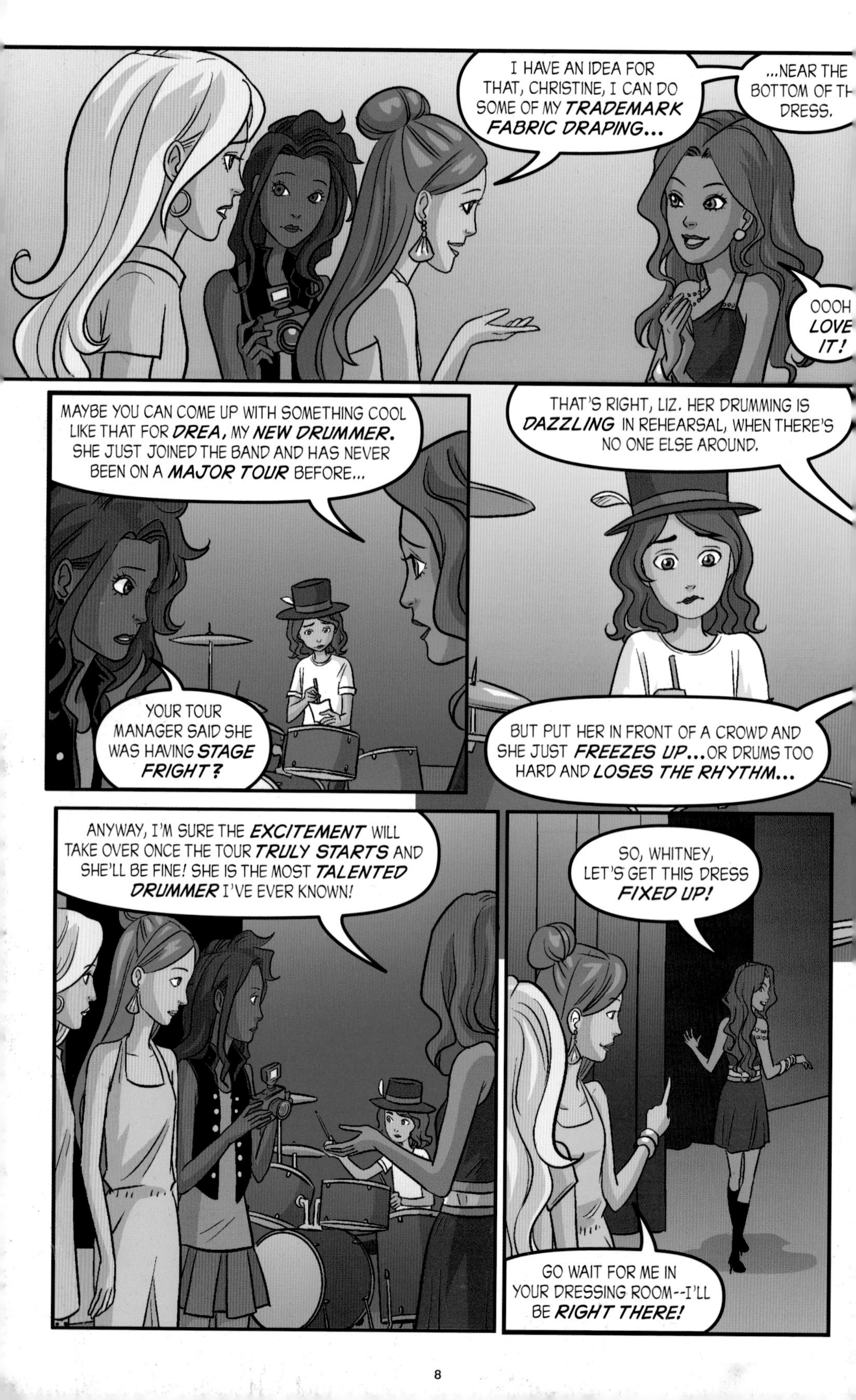
I HAVE AN IDEA FOR THAT, CHRISTINE, I CAN DO SOME OF MY TRADEMARK FABRIC DRAPING...
...NEAR THE BOTTOM OF TH DRESS.
OOOH LOVE IT!
MAYBE YOU CAN COME UP WITH SOMETHING COOL LIKE THAT FOR DREA, MY NEW DRUMMER. SHE JUST JOINED THE BAND AND HAS NEVER BEEN ON A MAJOR TOUR BEFORE...
YOUR TOUR MANAGER SAID SHE WAS HAVING STAGE FRIGHT?
THAT'S RIGHT, LIZ. HER DRUMMING IS DAZZLING IN REHEARSAL, WHEN THERE'S NO ONE ELSE AROUND.
BUT PUT HER IN FRONT OF A CROWD AND SHE JUST FREEZES UP...OR DRUMS TOO HARD AND LOSES THE RHYTHM...
ANYWAY, I'M SURE THE EXCITEMENT WILL TAKE OVER ONCE THE TOUR TRULY STARTS AND SHE'LL BE FINE! SHE IS THE MOST TALENTED DRUMMER I'VE EVER KNOWN!
SO, WHITNEY, LET'S GET THIS DRESS FIXED UP!
GO WAIT FOR ME IN YOUR DRESSING ROOM--I'LL BE RIGHT THERE!

WHAT'S GOING ON?
WHAT DO YOU MEAN?
YOU'RE NOT ACTING LIKE YOURSELF...
WHAT? THAT'S RIDICULOUS! OF COURSE I AM, I--
WHITNEY, BARBIE: WHICH ONE OF THESE GOES BEST WITH...
...MY OPENING NUMBER OUTFIT?
BARBIE, WHAT DO YOU THINK?
I...UH... ER...
WEAR THE GOLD.
IT POPS AGAINST THE COLOR SCHEME WE'RE USING.
AWESOME. THANK YOU!

OKAY, OKAY, YOU GOT ME!
YOU WERE SAYING...?
I'M SO EXCITED TO BE ON TOUR WITH CHRISTINE VEGA AND HER AMAZING BAND...AND TO BE ASSISTING YOU, WHITNEY...
BUT I'VE NEVER BEEN PART OF SOMETHING THIS BIG BEFORE.
MY NERVES ARE MAKING IT HARD TO CONNECT TO MY CREATIVITY. MY FASHION VISION FEELS BLURRY. I HAVEN'T DESIGNED ANYTHING NEW SINCE WE STARTED THE TOUR.
LIKE CHRISTINE'S DRUMMER, DREA--I KEEP FREEZING UP!
I HAVE DESIGNER'S BLOCK!

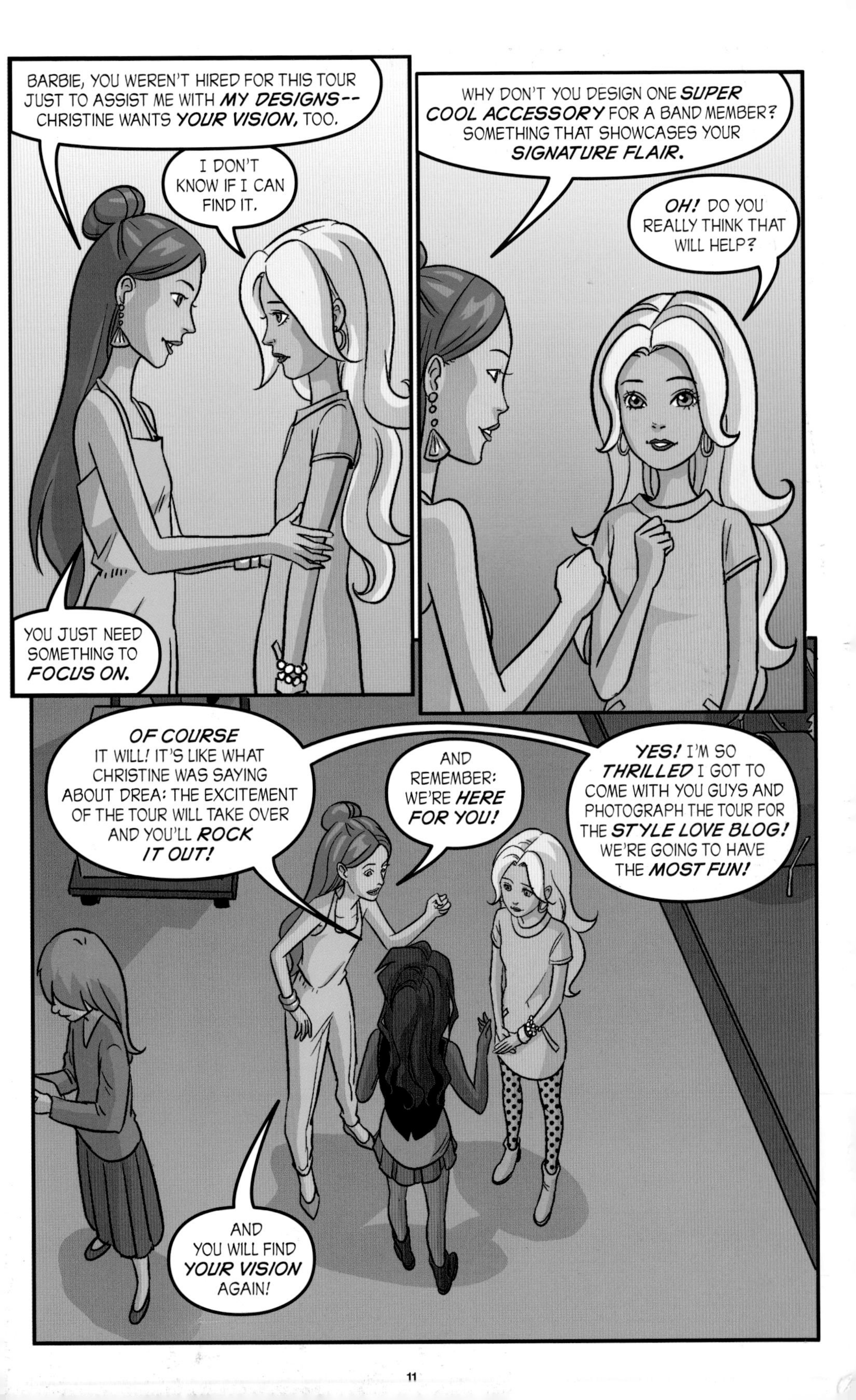
BARBIE, YOU WEREN'T HIRED FOR THIS TOUR JUST TO ASSIST ME WITH *MY DESIGNS*-- CHRISTINE WANTS *YOUR VISION,* TOO.
I DON'T KNOW IF I CAN FIND IT.
YOU JUST NEED SOMETHING TO *FOCUS ON.*
WHY DON'T YOU DESIGN ONE *SUPER COOL ACCESSORY* FOR A BAND MEMBER? SOMETHING THAT SHOWCASES YOUR *SIGNATURE FLAIR.*
OH! DO YOU REALLY THINK THAT WILL HELP?
OF COURSE IT WILL! IT'S LIKE WHAT CHRISTINE WAS SAYING ABOUT DREA: THE EXCITEMENT OF THE TOUR WILL TAKE OVER AND YOU'LL *ROCK IT OUT!*
AND REMEMBER: WE'RE *HERE FOR YOU!*
YES! I'M SO *THRILLED* I GOT TO COME WITH YOU GUYS AND PHOTOGRAPH THE TOUR FOR THE *STYLE LOVE BLOG!* WE'RE GOING TO HAVE THE *MOST FUN!*
AND YOU WILL FIND *YOUR VISION* AGAIN!

OH, I HOPE SO! THANKS FOR THE HEART-TO-HEART, GIRLS!
AS LONG AS WE'RE ALL HERE TOGETHER, THIS IS GOING TO BE THE BEST TOUR EVER!

LATER...
THIS IS SO EXCITING!
THE LAST DRESS REHEARSAL BEFORE OPENING NIGHT!
AND IN FRONT OF PRESS! HOPEFULLY THE TOUR WILL GET SOME GOOD COVERAGE...
SOMETHING'S WRONG...
THE BEAT IS OFF...

...rehearsal disaster...
...band not ready...
...tour marred by sour notes...
OOPS! NOT TO WORRY, EVERYONE! WE WERE JUST, UM...TRYING OUT A COOL NEW STUNT!
CLEARLY IT DIDN'T QUITE WORK...BUT WE'LL BE ALL READY FOR OPENING NIGHT TOMORROW! SEE YOU THEN!

WELL, THAT WAS... NOT GOOD.
IT WAS A DISASTER.
I HOPE CHRISTINE IS RIGHT. I HOPE DREA LOSES THE NERVES...AND FINDS HER RHYTHM.
POOR DREA.
YEAH, OTHERWISE THIS TOUR'S GOING TO BE RUINED BEFORE IT CAN EVEN GET STARTED!
WELL...WE BETTER GET A GOOD NIGHT'S SLEEP. TOMORROW'S THE BIG DAY!

THE NEXT DAY...
OPENING NIGHT!
BEST TOUR EVER!
RIGHT, BARBIE?
RIGHT! LET'S DO THIS!
SO I'LL MAKE SOME FINAL ADJUSTMENTS TO THE COSTUMES...
AND I'LL DOCUMENT THE WHOLE PROCESS FOR STYLE LOVE...
AND I'LL, UM...
DESIGN YOUR SUPER COOL ACCESSORY. RIGHT?
...RIGHT. IF I CAN GET OVER MY DESIGNER'S BLOCK!
IT'S WORSE THAN EVER...
BUMP

DREA... WHAT'S WRONG?
I CAN'T... I CAN'T DO IT...
CAN'T DO WHAT?
I CAN'T GO ON TONIGHT. I'LL LOSE THE RHYTHM AND RUIN EVERYTHING AGAIN. I HAVE TO QUIT THE TOUR.
QUIT? YOU CAN'T QUIT!
THERE'S NO ONE TO REPLACE YOU! IF YOU QUIT IT, WILL RUIN THE TOUR!
AND YOU SHOULDN'T GIVE UP ON YOUR DREAMS.
I DON'T KNOW WHAT TO DO.

WE'LL HELP YOU!
WE WILL?
WE CAN HELP, RIGHT? WE CAN SHOW HER THAT DREAMS ARE ALWAYS POSSIBLE! WE CAN MAKE THIS THE BEST TOUR EVER!
BUT HOW?
ESPECIALLY NOW... WHEN YOU'RE HAVING DESIGNER'S BLOCK?
I...HAVEN'T TOTALLY FIGURED THAT OUT YET! BUT I DO KNOW THIS: WE CAN SOLVE ANYTHING WITH TEAMWORK AND FRIENDSHIP!

WE'LL HELP YOU...
BUT HAVEN'T TOTALLY FIGURED OUT HOW YET!
BUT WE WILL!

I'VE GOT IT!
YOU NEED A BETTER OPENING NIGHT COSTUME!
WE GAVE CHRISTINE THE FLASHIEST OSTUMES AND KEPT THE BAND MEMBERS' OUTFITS MORE UNDERSTATED...
BUT IF WE GIVE YOU JUST A BIT MORE PIZZAZZ...
...MAYBE YOU'LL FEEL AS CONFIDENT AS CHRISTINE ALWAYS DOES!
...AND CONFIDENCE WILL HELP YOU FIND YOUR RHYTHM AGAIN!

SOMETHING WITH FLAIR...
SOMETHING WITH DRAMA...
SOMETHING THAT WILL MAKE A STATEMENT...
PUT IT ALL TOGETHER...
...AND YOU GET...

THE PERFECT OUTFIT!

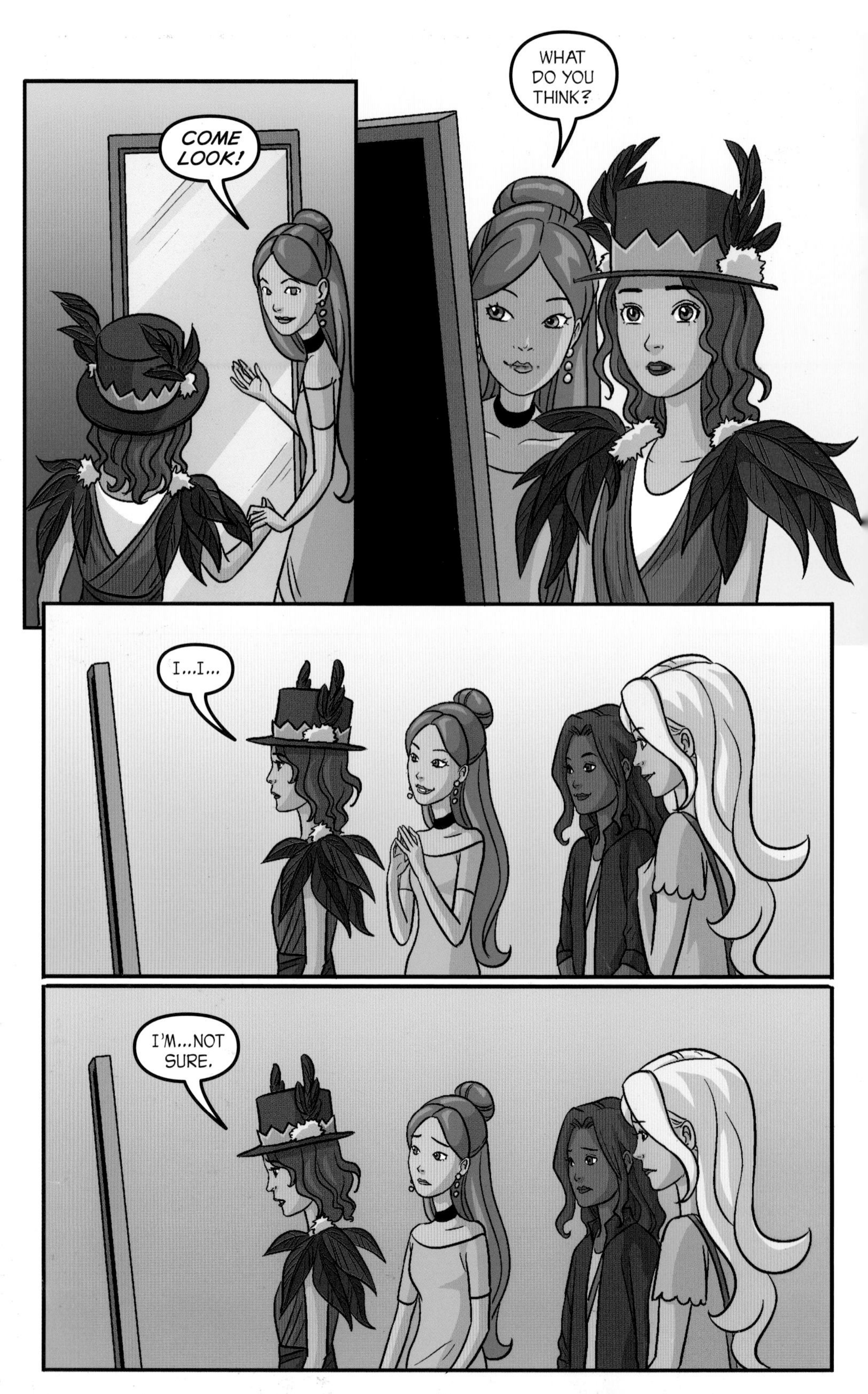
COME LOOK!
WHAT DO YOU THINK?
I...I...
I'M...NOT SURE.

BARBIE! MAYBE IF YOU DESIGN A SUPER COOL ACCESSORY TO GO WITH THE OUTFIT, IT WILL HELP!
UH... OKAY...
MAYBE IF I JUST...

DRAPE
TWIST
ROLL
FOLD
IT'S NO USE! MY *DESIGNER'S BLOCK* HAS TAKEN OVER!

I HAVE AN IDEA!
MAYBE YOU NEED TO SEE PEOPLE'S REACTIONS TO THIS FABULOUS OUTFIT!
THERE'S A CROWD JUST OUTSIDE THE STAGE DOOR--SOME FANS, SOME PRESS. ALL HOPING TO GET A GLIMPSE OF CHRISTINE AND THE BAND.
C-CROWD?
LIZ AND I WILL GO OUT WITH YOU. WE'LL BE THERE EVERY STEP OF THE WAY!

STAGE DOOR
YOU LOOK AMAZING!
YES! EVERYONE OUT THERE IS GOING TO LOVE YOUR COSTUME!
READY?
OKAY.
YES.
LET'S DO THIS!

HEY, ISN'T THAT CHRISTINE'S NEW DRUMMER?!
IT IS!
DREA! HER NAME IS DREA!
FLASH
CLIK
FLASH
FLASH
CLIK
FLASH
CLIK
DREA! OVER HERE!
DID YOU HEAR...
...FROZE UP DURING REHEARSAL...
FLASH
FLASH
FLASH
CLIK
CLIK
FLASH
...THREW A DRUMSTICK...
CLIK
FLASH
FLASH
FLASH
CLIK
...TOTAL DISASTER...
CLIK
FLASH
CLIK
FLASH
FLASH
CLIK
TELL US ABOUT THE DRUMSTICK!
DREA!
DREA!
DREA!

FLASH
I CAN'T!
FLASH
FLASH
FLASH
FLASH
FLASH
FLASH
FLASH
SH
RIPPPPPPPP
FLASH
FLASH
FLASH
CLIK
CLIK
FLASH
FLASH
CLIK
FLASH

WHAT HAPPENED OUT THERE? SHE'S SO UPSET, I CAN'T GET HER TO TELL ME.
OUR CONFIDENCE THROUGH COSTUMES PLAN MAY HAVE MISSED THE MARK.
I WISH WE COULD FIGURE OUT HOW TO HELP HER...
WHAT'S SHE DOING?

TING
TING
TING
BOOOM
BADA
BOOOOM
BADA
BOOM
WOW... SHE'S AMAZING!

BADABOOOOM
BOOoom
BADA BOOM
BOOOM
STRUMMM
TWANNG
BADA BOOoOM
BOOOM

BOOOM
STRUMM
STRUMM
BADA BOOM
BOOoom
THRUMMM
THRUM
TING

BADA BOOM
BOOOOM
TWANNG
STRUMMM
STRUMMM
TWANNNG
BADA BOOOOOM
BOOOOM

BADA BOOM
TWANNG
CLAP
CLAP
CLAP
CLAP
CLAP
CLAP
CLAP
CLAP
CLAP
CLAP

YAY!
CLAP
CLAP
WOOHOO!
CLAP
CLAP
CLAP
CLAP
AWESOME!
CLAP
ENCORE!
ENCORE!
CLAP
ENCORE!
CLAP

ENCORE! ENCORE! ENCORE!
I...I CAN'T!
CLATTER
CLATTER
SORRY, GUYS-- JUST A LITTLE IMPROMPTU JAM SESSION!
WE SHOULD PROBABLY ALL GET BACK TO WORK...
I SHOULD HAVE QUIT. I'M GOING TO RUIN EVERYTHING...
NO! WE JUST HAVEN'T FOUND THE RIGHT SOLUTION TO BOOST YOUR CONFIDENCE. BUT WE WILL!

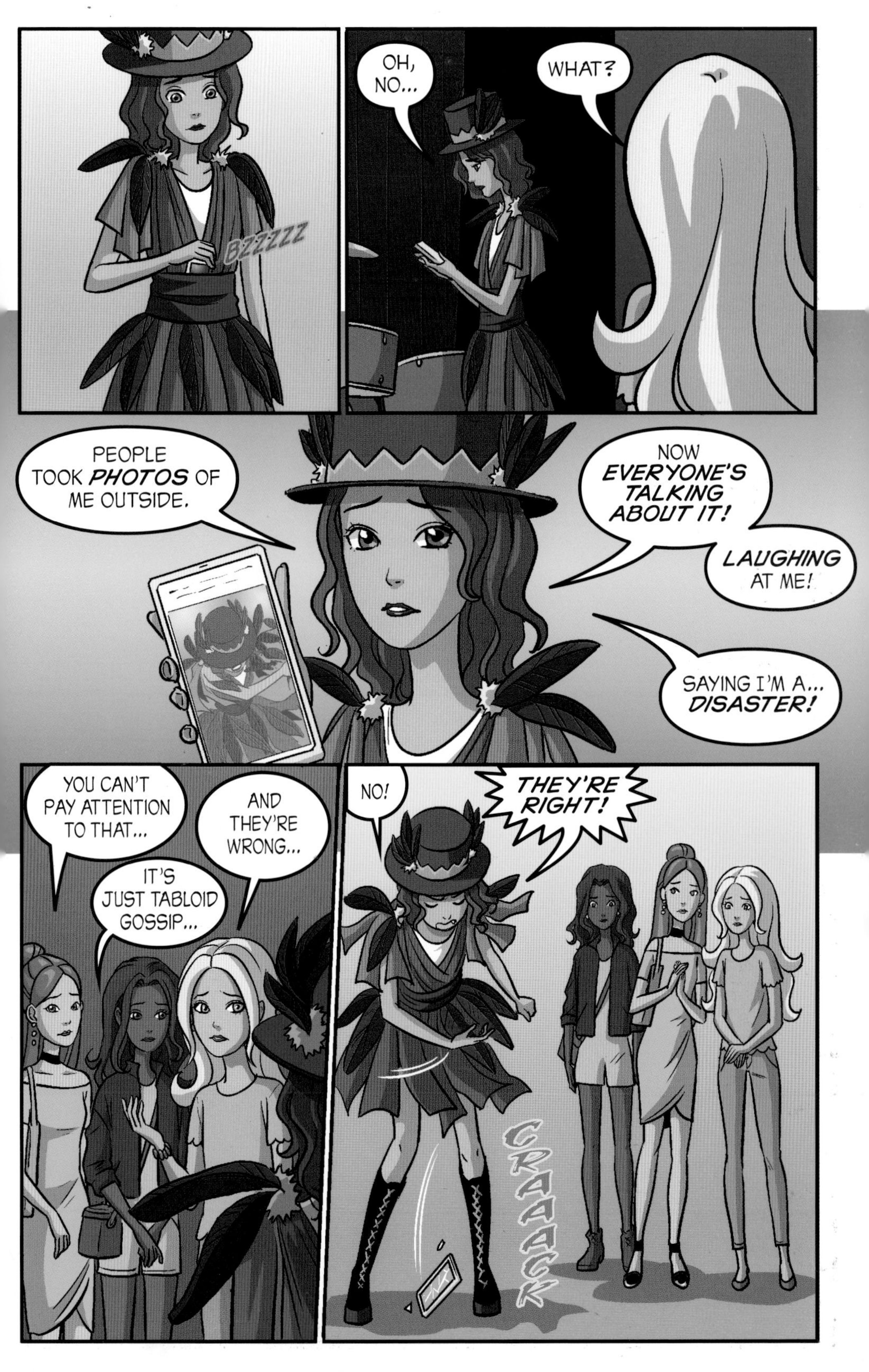
BZZZZZ
OH, NO...
WHAT?
PEOPLE TOOK *PHOTOS* OF ME OUTSIDE.
NOW *EVERYONE'S TALKING ABOUT IT!*
LAUGHING AT ME!
SAYING I'M A... *DISASTER!*
YOU CAN'T PAY ATTENTION TO THAT...
IT'S JUST TABLOID GOSSIP...
AND THEY'RE WRONG...
NO!
THEY'RE RIGHT!
CRAAACK

I THOUGHT I COULD DO THIS... BUT I JUST CAN'T!
I WISH I LOVED OUTRAGEOUS COSTUMES AND BIG CROWDS LIKE CHRISTINE...
DREA...
...BUT I JUST DON'T!
PLEASE...
WHENEVER I SEE A LOT OF PEOPLE WATCHING ME PLAY...
...A LOT OF PEOPLE WATCHING ME DO ANYTHING, I FREEZE UP!
I THOUGHT I COULD FIND MY CONFIDENCE, BUT MY STAGE FRIGHT IS WORSE THAN EVER!
WATCH OUT!
I JUST-- WHOA!

GRAAAAAASH
THAT'S IT...
I QUIT!

I THOUGHT WE COULD HELP HER...
THAT WE COULD BRING OUT HER CONFIDENCE...
BUT WE DIDN'T.
AND NOW THE TOUR REALLY IS RUINED.
THIS IS MOST DEFINITELY NOT THE BEST TOUR EVER. IT'S THE OPPOSITE OF THAT.

AND I STILL HAVE DESIGNER'S BLOCK.
HOW DID EVERYTHING GO SO WRONG?
WHAT'S THIS? NOTES?
AHHH, YES...THOSE MUST BE WHAT DREA WAS SCRIBBLING TO HERSELF DURING REHEARSAL?

"FORGET THE CROWD, FIND YOURSELF."
FIND YOURSELF... OF COURSE.
I KNOW HOW WE CAN HELP DREA!

DREA
DREA
I THINK I SHOULD TRY TALKING TO HER *MYSELF*.
GO FOR IT.
GOOD LUCK.

HI...
I'M NOT CHANGING MY MIND!
I'M SORRY.
WHITNEY, LIZ, AND I...WE FOCUSED ON THINGS THAT WOULD GIVE CHRISTINE CONFIDENCE.
NOT THINGS THAT WOULD GIVE YOU CONFIDENCE.
OR FIT WITH YOUR STYLE.
BUT SEEING YOU PLAY DRUMS JUST NOW...I SAW THE REAL YOU.
THE YOU WHO DEEPLY LOVES MUSIC, CONNECTS TO MUSIC...
THAT INSPIRED ME.

AND YOUR NOTE INSPIRED ME EVEN MORE.
SEEING THIS...I THINK IT BROKE MY DESIGNER'S BLOCK.
I THINK I KNOW HOW TO HELP YOU WITH YOUR STAGE FRIGHT... IF YOU'LL LET ME.

WOW... OPENING NIGHT IS FINALLY HERE...
LOOK AT ALL THESE PEOPLE...
IT'S COMPLETELY SOLD OUT...
WHITNEY! I'M SO EXCITED TO FINALLY SHOW OFF YOUR DESIGNS!
BUT, BARBIE... I WAS REALLY HOPING WE'D SEE MORE OF YOUR UNIQUE FLAIR IN THE COSTUMES.
OH... YOU JUST MIGHT...

OH, REALLY? WELL, THEN... I CAN'T WAIT!
THE ONLY THING I HAVE LEFT TO WORRY ABOUT IS MY DRUMMER.
I THOUGHT SHE WAS GOING TO QUIT...BUT SHE ASSURED ME SHE'D BE FINE.
BUT AFTER YESTERDAY'S REHEARSAL MISHAPS, I JUST DON'T KNOW...
I THINK YOU MIGHT BE SURPRISED...
BY WHAT?
THAT.

WOW!

HOW DO YOU FEEL?
DREA! YOU LOOK AMAZING! I LOVE THE VEIL!
I FEEL AMAZING. I FEEL LIKE ME.
OKAY, LET'S TRY THE FINAL TEST...
WHEN YOU LOOK OUT AT THE CROWD, HOW DO YOU FEEL? IS THE VEIL WORKING?
YES. IT'S PERFECT.
IT SOFTENS THE OVERWHELMING EFFECT OF THE CROWD. I FEEL LIKE I CAN JUST GET IN TOUCH WITH MY MUSIC...
...AND PLAY. LIKE I CAN FIND MY RHYTHM AGAIN.

THANK YOU.
THANKS TO ALL OF YOU. FOR HELPING ME. FOR BELIEVING IN ME.
NOW LET'S ROCK!
BARBIE! THAT VEIL IS BRILLIANT -- THE PERFECT SUPER COOL ACCESSORY!
YOU TOTALLY WORKED THROUGH YOUR DESIGNER'S BLOCK!
WHEN DREA AND I WERE PLAYING TOGETHER...SEEING HER RECONNECT WITH HER LOVE OF MUSIC HELPED ME RECONNECT WITH MY LOVE OF DESIGN.
JUST LIKE SHE FOUND HER RHYTHM AGAIN... I FOUND MY VISION AGAIN.
AND YOU GUYS WERE THERE FOR ME EVERY STEP OF THE WAY! I COULDN'T HAVE WORKED THROUGH IT WITHOUT MY FRIENDS!

BARBIE! WHITNEY! LIZ! COME ON OUT HERE!
LET'S GIVE IT UP FOR THESE GIRLS--THEY SAVED MY TOUR!
THIS IS AMAZING!
INCREDIBLE!
I CAN'T BELIEVE IT!
AND WE'RE FINALLY HAVING...

THE BEST TOUR EVER!
THE END

WATCH OUT FOR PAPERCUTZ

Welcome to the simply sensational second BARBIE graphic novel from Papercutz, those fashion forward folks dedicated to publishing great graphic novels for all ages. I'm Jim Salicrup, Editor-in-Chief. Wait, did we say "second"? Well, technically this is BARBIE #2, but there have been a couple of other great BARBIE graphic novels published recently that are still available at your favorite bookseller or library.

One is called BARBIE PUPPY PARTY and it features an all-new story by Danica Davidson, writer and Maria Victoria Robado, artist, starring Barbie, her sisters Skipper, Stacie, and Chelsea, and their pets Honey, Rookie, Taffy, and DJ. Barbie and her sisters are organizing an adoption event for the local animal shelter, but it's scheduled on the same day as the puppies' birthday. The Puppies think they're being forgotten, but that can't be, can it? The surprising answer awaits you within BARBIE PUPPY PARTY.

Barbie pursues a career in the pages of BARBIE, she spends time with her family and pets in BARBIE PUPPY PARTY, and has an out-of-this-world experience in BARBIE STAR LIGHT ADVENTURE. Barbie's not just a princess in this special graphic novel, she's Princess Star Light, from the planet Para-Den. When she discovers someone is trying to destroy the environment, Barbie and her friends, Sal-Lee (a hoverboard racing legend), Sheena and Kareena (Gravity Geniuses), and Leo (Prince and pilot) work together to save the planet they love.

But wait, there's more! Coming soon is BARBIE #3 in which Barbie faces all-new exciting challanges and in BARBIE VIDEO GAME HERO, we see Barbie as an all-out action hero! All these graphic novels simply prove you can be anything! For more news about upcoming BARBIE graphic novels, be sure to visit Papercutz.com.

Jim

STAY IN TOUCH!

EMAIL: salicrup@papercutz.com
WEB: papercutz.com
TWITTER: @papercutzgn
INSTAGRAM: @papercutzgn
FACEBOOK: PAPERCUTZGRAPHICNOVELS
FANMAIL: Papercutz, 160 Broadway, Suite 700
East Wing, New York, NY 10038

...AAAAND LANDING COURSE IS SET! VACATION IMMINENT.
PARA-DEN IS THE *PERFECT* VACATION PLACE!
PLACES TO HOVERBOARD...
...OPEN FIELDS FOR PILOTING TRICKS...
AND PLENTY OF--
...BRIGHTLY COLORED FOLIAGE?
...GREAT VIEWS FROM UP HIGH?

HAHA, YES! HOW'D YOU GUESS?
WHAT ELSE--
--WOULD GET US SO EXCITED?
OKAY, EVERYONE. HOLD TIGHT. WE'RE COMING IN FOR A LANDING!
"WE'LL GO AROUND TO AVOID THE FOG!"

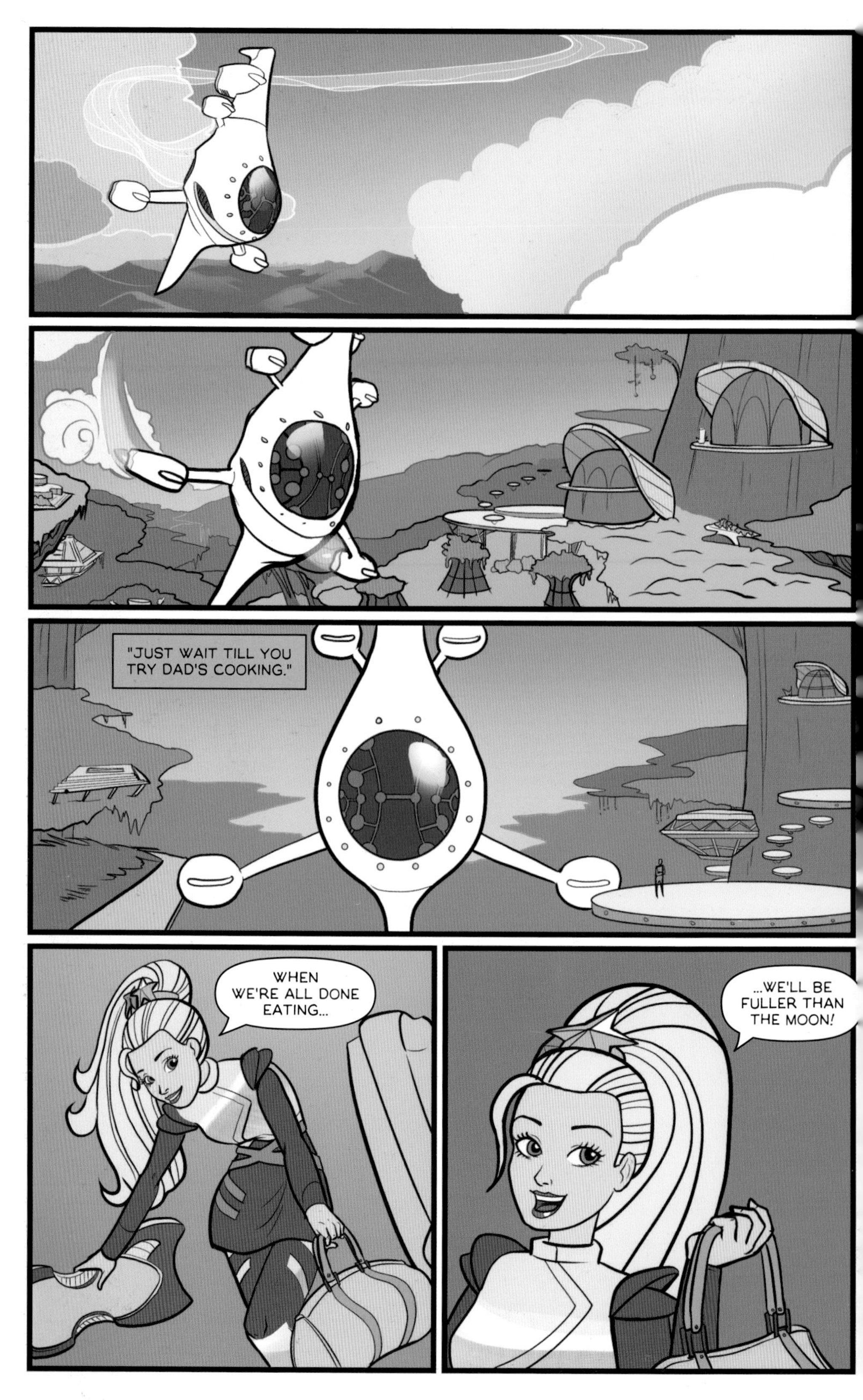
"JUST WAIT TILL YOU TRY DAD'S COOKING."
WHEN WE'RE ALL DONE EATING...
...WE'LL BE FULLER THAN THE MOON!

MMMM!
SOUNDS AMAZING!
THUNK

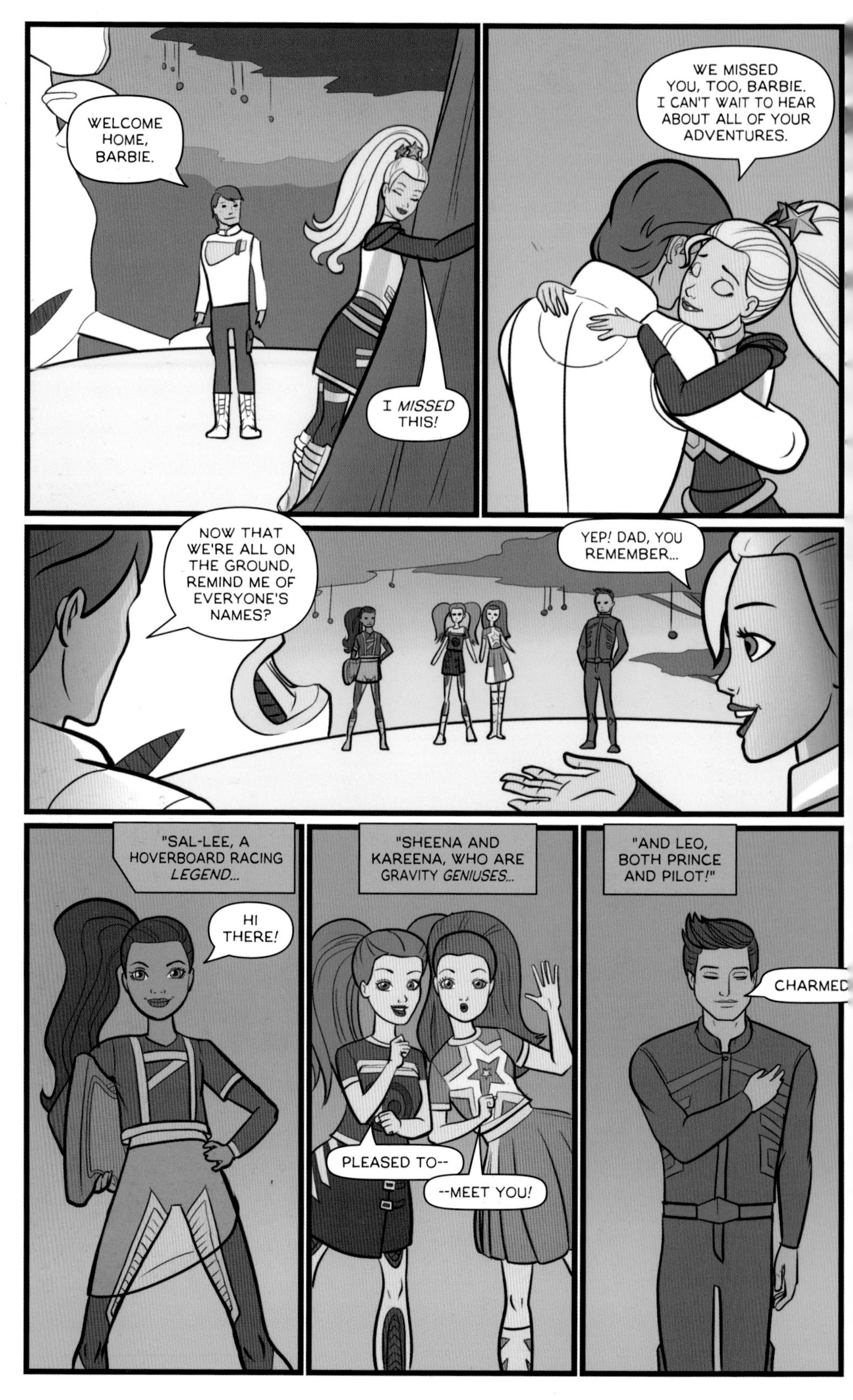
WELCOME HOME, BARBIE.
I *MISSED* THIS!
WE MISSED YOU, TOO, BARBIE. I CAN'T WAIT TO HEAR ABOUT ALL OF YOUR ADVENTURES.
NOW THAT WE'RE ALL ON THE GROUND, REMIND ME OF EVERYONE'S NAMES?
YEP! DAD, YOU REMEMBER...
"SAL-LEE, A HOVERBOARD RACING *LEGEND*...
HI THERE!
"SHEENA AND KAREENA, WHO ARE GRAVITY *GENIUSES*...
PLEASED TO--
--MEET YOU!
"AND LEO, BOTH PRINCE AND PILOT!"
CHARMED

AND YOU'RE ALL ABOUT TO EXPERIENCE MY DAD'S ***AMAZING*** COOKING FIRST HAND! HE'S THE BEST IN THIS GALAXY...OR ANY OTHER.
THAT'S GOOD NEWS!
GURRRGLE
I COULD GO FOR A HOME-COOKED MEAL!
GEMBERRY CASSEROLE, POMEGRANATE SALAD, BLACK BEAN TENDERS...
WELL, COME ON IN, I'VE BEEN COOKING ALL DAY!

GALACTIMANGO PUNCH *FLOATS*, FIREFLY PIE, AAAAND NACHOS!
DIG IN!
ER, DAD...
WE WERE ALL *REALLY* EXCITED TO EXPLORE PARA-DEN. MAYBE...WE COULD MAKE IT A PICNIC?
THAT'S A ***GREAT*** IDEA! I JUST GOT A NEW BLANKET! FOOD'S BETTER OUT IN NATURE!
PHEW! I WAS GONNA HAVE TO HOVERBOARD IN THE HALL IF I DIDN'T GET OUTSIDE SOON. SHIPS MAKE ME STIR-CRAZY!

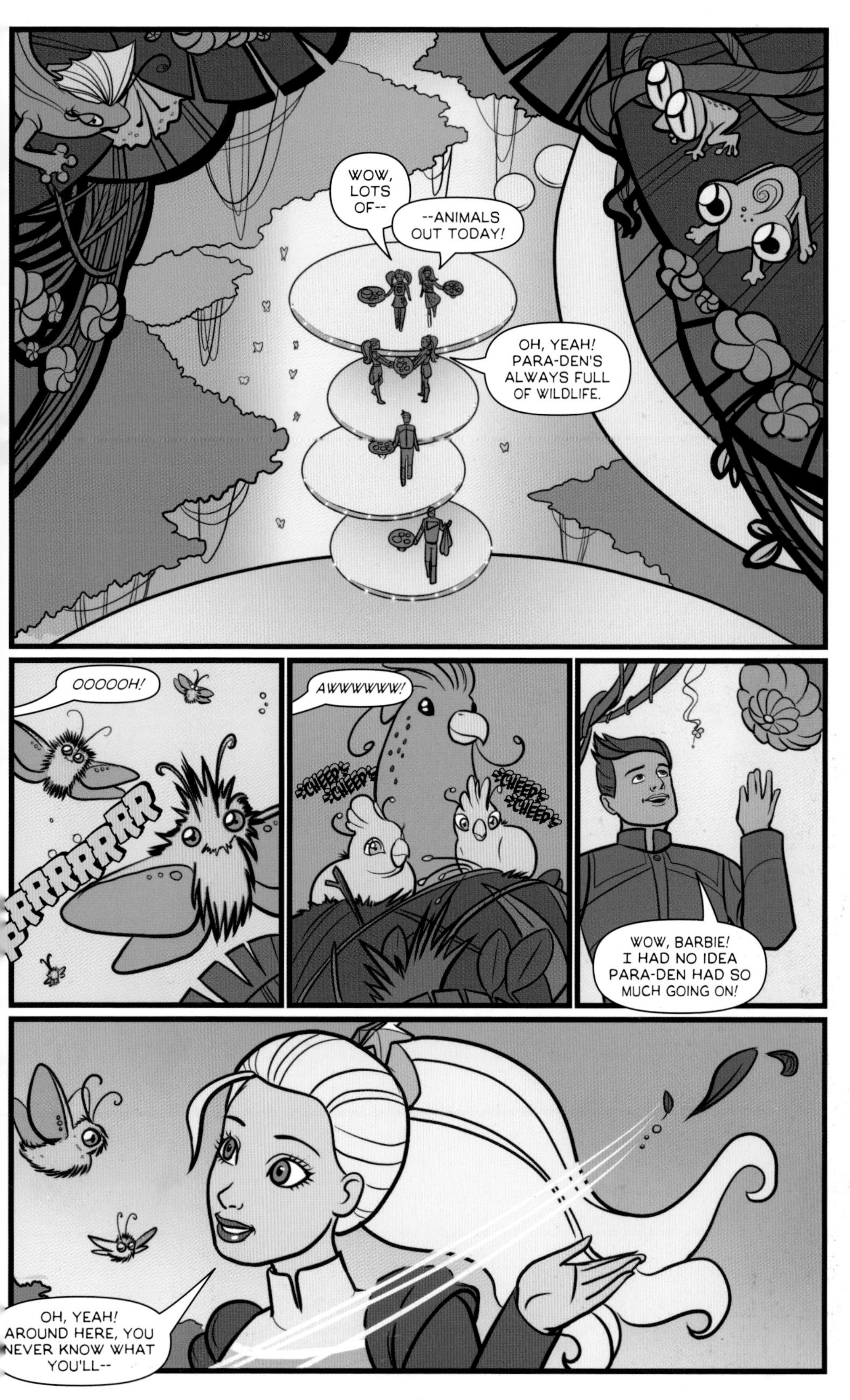
WOW, LOTS OF--
--ANIMALS OUT TODAY!
OH, YEAH! PARA-DEN'S ALWAYS FULL OF WILDLIFE.
OOOOOH!
PRRRRRRR
AWWWWWW!
CHEEP CHEEP
CHEEP CHEEP
WOW, BARBIE! I HAD NO IDEA PARA-DEN HAD SO MUCH GOING ON!
OH, YEAH! AROUND HERE, YOU NEVER KNOW WHAT YOU'LL--

--SEE!?
WHAT HAPPENED TO THE FOREST?
THE FOG HAS BEEN SO BAD, I COULDN'T SEE A THING! I CAME HERE ON MY WALK JUST LAST WEEK! I DIDN'T SEE ANYTHING.
HEY, AREN'T THERE SUPPOSED TO BE TREES HERE?
VROOOM
BEEP BEEP
CRASH
I GREW UP IN THIS FOREST. I RODE MY FIRST HOVERBOARD HERE!
I GOTTA STOP THIS.
Don't miss BARBIE STAR LIGHT ADVENTURE "The Secret of the Gems," available now at booksellers everywhere!